In The Realm of The Magic Ruby

VLADIMIRA KUNA

ORIGINAL STORY TOLD BY MARIE CALMA

ILLUSTRATED BY YORRIS HANDOKO

Published by
Hasmark Publishing
www.hasmarkpublishing.com

Permission should be addressed in writing to vladi@vladimirakuna.com
Editors: Alison Burney, Gena West, Renata Natale and Claire Roberts

Cover Designer: Vladimira Kuna designed, Yorris Handoko illustrated
Illustrator: Yorris Handoko

Layout Artists: Vladimira Kuna, Yorris Handoko and Trace Haskins

ISBN 13: 978-1-77482-209-8
ISBN 10: 1774822091

I dedicate this book
to my beautifully abundant and open-minded
children and nephew

Joshua, Elizabeth & Tobias

and all the children in the world.

***

*I intend for your imagination and persistence
to manifest anything you desire.*

***

Endorsements

"This fairy-tale, written for all ages, provides a wonderful understanding of the true gifts in life. The story captivates, inspires and takes you on an exceptional journey of discovery. Allow yourself to be swept away in the land of make believe. You may find that you truly enjoy the experience."

Peggy McColl, New York Times Best-Selling Author

***

"When Vladi told me about this book I immediately wanted to read it. What I was happy to discover is that this was not just a book about a long forgotten in Czech fairy-tale but something truly wonderful. This is for both children and adults and it demonstrates pure love, the power of dreamig big, and the importance of vision and faith regardless of where you are in life.

Pick up this book. You won't be sorry and you'll be in for the ride of your life."

Phillip Goldfine, Academy Award Winning Hollywood Producer

***

"This fairy-tale is entertaining and has great characters. Its descriptions set the imagination to work. It tells of the struggles of a young boy who endures hardship and blessings and works through the confusion of loyalty, love, and magic. Yet its ending is full of hope. This tale is great for children and the adults who read to them - just as Anderson said stories should be. "

Michelle Snyder, Author, Symbology Expert
and Founder & VP of Enzmann Archives

"This is a delightful fairy-tale about hope and what happens when you come into contact with 'angels' who are willing to help you. In this case, a group of dwarfs, who assist a tired and lonely young man to once again, dream. In the beginning, most of them see helping him as their gain, however, one dwarf understands the boy on a much deeper level and proceeds to do in selflessness what the other dwarfs fail to see. The boy learns to trust and in the process, finds his own special love. The one requirement is that he must leave his past behind in order to be able to enjoy the world around him in all its fullness. An expansive story for children and adults alike."

Renata Natale, Author of Casting Away:
Adventures of A Dead Man

***

"In The Realm of The Magic Ruby is a story filled with adventure, empathy, curiosity, temptation, desire, courage, love and integrity – and beautifully demonstrates how challenges and mistakes can lead to divine and beautiful endings ... which I might add ... are really new beginnings. As a Father, I love the lessons this book teaches kids and adults alike! Thank you, Vladimira, for bringing this gift to the world's spotlight."

Trace Haskins, Author of Prosperous On Purpose

***

"In The Realm of The Magic Ruby, is an engaging tale of love, truth, forgiveness, and magic. It is beautifully illustrated and will be enjoyed by children many times over, who will appreciate the timeless message - that love is the greatest treasure of all."

Heather Lean, Bestselling Author of Angel Grandma,
God Hears My Song, and Isn't It a Miracle?

"In the Realm of the Magic Ruby, is a captivating fairy tale full of essential life lessons which will inspire any parent and child to believe in the unseen magic that is all around us. This beautifully illustrated and creatively written fairytale delivers the magic of installing empowering thoughts, faith and supportive beliefs that will last a lifetime. A must for any parent or child to read together and co-create a life full of joy, abundance and gratitude."

Roddy Telfer, Business, Mindset and Marketing Coach

***

"In 'The Realm of The Magic Ruby', we are reminded of the power of doing the right thing, even in the face of temptation and pressure. Through the compelling story of Aaron, a boy who makes a mistake but ultimately finds the courage to correct it, we learn valuable lessons about honesty, integrity, and the importance of standing up for what is right.

The characters in this tale are relatable and endearing, from the demanding dwarf who leads Aaron astray to the kind and generous princess whose forgiveness and love inspire him to make amends. The journey of Aaron's transformation from a misguided boy to a noble hero is one that will stay with readers long after the final pages are turned.

Whether you're a child learning the importance of honesty or an adult who needs a reminder of the value of doing what is right, 'In The Realm of The Magic Ruby' is a must-read. This story is a testament to the enduring power of honesty, integrity, and forgiveness, and it is sure to touch the hearts of readers of all ages."

Norman Gräter, International Multi Award Winning Mindset Speaker & Gamechanger

It was a peaceful night in the enchanted woodland. The soft blue moonlight spread a blanket of sparkling glitter across the forest floor. Just as midnight approached, six dwarfs almost invisibly jumped out of hiding through the enormous fern bushes and landed on the soft moss.

They carefully checked every part of the opening, every loophole, every nook and every possible means of escape to ensure no hidden gap existed. Once they felt sure there was no living soul hiding in the surroundings, and there was no heartbeat to be heard, they sat down in the beautiful, fresh-smelling moss.

Discussions on which little nightly jaunt beckoned them were accompanied by excitement for this next adventure. Their positive-vibrating energies filled every interspace, leaving sparkles of gold on everything they touched.

The oldest, wisest dwarf began to tell his story first. He gently brushed his silver sparkling beard with grizzled fingers and said in a deep, serene voice:

"Last night, I crept up all the way to the king's castle. Beautiful ladies and gentlemen were dancing and laughing. Music and laughter filled the air. Everyone felt blessed to have such a great feast. I noticed the people were adorned with sparkling jewels, stunning gold and tiaras. Out of them all, shining far above the rest, was the most magnificent jewel sitting on the stunning black hair of the king's daughter, Zora. This beautiful princess wore the most extraordinary ruby I have ever seen. I want to get this for our underground treasure box."

The oldest dwarf, whose beard sparkled like pure silver, paused. The youngest dwarf waved his hand to take the next turn. He was charming and handsome with curly golden hair, and he was full of courage; the bravest of them all.

"I also saw the stunning ruby and I happen to know where its hiding place is."

All the dwarfs clapped their hands excitedly, using their vivid imaginations to visualize this magnificent stone.

"The princess only takes it off when brushing her stunning black hair," continued the youngest dwarf.

"She puts the ruby down on a silver plate and does not let it out of her sight. It is said to be a charming jewel with magic powers. The story says that whoever possesses the ruby and carries it awakens its magic, which allows them to understand and talk to flowers, plants, trees and leaves. All the magic of the world will be revealed to that person."

Suddenly, the sound of broken twigs emerged from the bushes near the forest, disturbing the dwarfs' gathering, and they all scattered in every possible direction.

A young boy wakes up, looking puzzled, but is amazed to find this little magical creature next to him. He feels calm and peaceful but is astonished when the smallest dwarf summons the other five and they appear in a flash out of nowhere. They encircle the boy and chatter enthusiastically, telling him all about the breakfast feast they prepared while he was asleep. The dwarfs present the food, which the starving boy graciously receives, still watching them with a hint of distrust. He begins to realise that these magical creatures will not harm him, so he slowly starts talking to them.

He explains how he left home to look for luck somewhere far away in the world. His voice reveals the pain in his heart as he tells of how he lost his beloved parents and has nothing left — no joy, no food, no help, and no home. He now lives in poverty. The dwarfs' eyes shed tears as big as peas. They promise to protect the boy, to love him and do all in their power to help him feel joy again.

They started competing to show their kindness and demonstrate their love. Their desire to make him happy and joyful was so strong. They took the curious boy down to their underground treasure room and showed him the hidden prized possessions, allowing him to choose whatever he wanted.

The dwarfs introduced him to the absolute beauty of the underground magic garden. They prepared a fragrant bath for him filled with rose petals of various colours and presented him with blue satin clothes, which made him look like a prince. Now that he was ready, they asked him if he wished to stay with them in the underground. They had only one condition: he could not return back to the world of the living.

The boy, whose name was Aaron, accepted the condition and swore not to return to the world from which he came. He felt so blessed to belong somewhere and was incredibly happy to stay with the dwarfs.

He had nothing above ground to look forward to, not a single memory filled with light. After his parents' death, his only companions were poverty and injustice.

Aaron's life underground was magical. Each new adventure filled him with delight and immense fulfilment. His curious mind was fascinated to learn and discover this novel land. He was surrounded by mystical creatures and animals he had never seen before. The land of dwarfs was made of crystals and gold. Beautiful, sparkling jewels shone in every corner of his new home. Diamonds hung from the ceilings, shining their beauty on everyone who entered the enchanted land of the dwarfs. Fragrant, iridescent flowers stood proud, powerfully tall, reminding Aaron of towering, strong trees.

And at night-time, when all the living creatures drifted off to sleep and the magic blue moonlight covered the glade again, Aaron accompanied the dwarfs on their visits to his living world, the Earth.

He would wait for them in the forest, hiding obediently as promised, until they returned for him. He was not allowed to go with them on treasure-hunting expeditions, so he came up with various ways to amuse himself while he waited.

He would shoot arrows into tree trunks or chase fireflies and gently catch them in his palms. However, the longer he lived underground, the more he longed to feel the sun's rays again. He longed to run and feel the wind while walking in the village, fields and forests. He longed to see a town and people.

This strange and magical land underground was a place where shining diamonds and jewels replaced the sun's warm rays. It was a place where creatures slithered all over the floor, brought to life by magic powers; nothing like the running, living animals on Earth. The powerful, tall flowers were no longer astonishing to Aaron. He wanted to see, smell and feel tall earthly trees and the whistling wind that rustled the leaves, creating magical music for his ears.

10

How he longed to run in a field full of the beautiful smell of natural flowers and just lie down in its centre, wide-eyed and dreaming in the middle of the day.

He wanted to escape the mystical underworld; this world filled with magic was one he no longer desired to be in. The Earth was far more beautiful and warm-hearted, and he longed to return to the land of the living. That was real-life magic, and he missed its beauty.

Every day he felt less joy, and his sad face started worrying his little companions. The dwarfs tried to make him happy by recounting all the funny stories from their escapades and bringing him presents and jewels… but nothing helped light up Aaron's soul.

Aaron's sadness grew and so did his craving to return to Earth. The smallest golden-haired dwarf wanted to know the reason for the boy's sadness, and once cried so much that Aaron shared his secret, expressing his wish to go back. The little dwarf shook his head and promised Aaron that he would return for him when all the others had taken off on their adventure. "I will come back for you and take you with me," he said.

Aaron felt ever so grateful to the smallest dwarf and his heart jumped for joy. He promised not to tell the others. The secret was safe with him.

At the usual witching hour, the enormous ferns opened the passage to the dwarfs and their comrade/companion. They all came out of hiding onto the moonlit glade. They checked every corner of the opening carefully, searching for hidden breaches. They left Aaron behind, in hiding as usual, and set off on their treasure hunt.

In a short while, the smallest curly-haired dwarf returned for the boy as promised. He grabbed his hand and pulled him through a tiny winding passage between the rocks, leaving the forest. Not too far away from them stood a magnificent castle made of marble and silver. The blue moonlight made it shine like a star and the alluring smell of flowers travelled from the surrounding gardens all the way to Aaron. He froze, mesmerised by the vision of the castle. Only when the dwarf pulled his sleeve several times did he come around and follow him further.

Aaron felt wonderful as the dwarf led him straight to the castle. They reached the city wall and sneaked in through a broken loophole, jumped on the branches of a massive oak tree, and slid down the mist straight into the park.

They had taken only a few steps when a noise in the distance alarmed them. Quickly, they hid behind the large trunk of the oak tree and waited quietly for the passerby to vanish.

The bright full moon lit up the passage and the entire green field in the park. A small lake full of lotus flowers sat in the middle. The sound of beautiful music coming from the bottom of the deep lake filled the air and sweet songs accompanied the ripples.

The boy stood breathless and felt the magical scene permeate his being. His amazement was indescribable when a stunning girl appeared. She looked like a magical fairy dancing next to the lake, undoing her beautiful long black tresses, which covered her silhouette like curly waves.

Once they were at the end of the forest passage leading to the glade where the entrance to the dwarfs' magic land was hidden under the enormous fern leaves, Aaron inquired about the beautiful girl. She had danced like a fairy and sang so stunningly that it captured his heart.

The dwarf did not want to answer, but he couldn`t refuse the plaintive pleading and gave in, letting the boy in on the secret. He told him about Princess Zora, the youngest daughter of the king of the marble castle. He then told him all about the magic jewel that sits in the princess's golden tiara—the ruby that reveals all the hidden secrets and imparts the power to understand the language of all flowers and leaves to the one who wears it.

He also mentioned that the oldest dwarf desires this magic ruby for himself, and how the little dwarf has been appointed to steal the jewel for him when the princess puts it down unnoticed.

"I am willing to steal that jewel for you!" said the boy eagerly.

The smallest dwarf liked the idea and immediately started to think of many ways this could be done. In the dead of night, the dwarf came up with a perfect plan and shared the details with Aaron before they arrived at the glade.

"There is another ball in the castle today. I will dress you up like a prince using our finest clothes from our underground dressing room, and I will give you the finest jewels out of our treasure collection. When you arrive at the castle, you will ask the princess for a dance. Once the dance is over, take the princess for a walk through the park. I will give you a special necklace covered in the shiniest diamonds. You will show this to her, and she will fall in love with it and demand it. You will offer to trade it for her ruby that sits so beautifully in her hair. And if she refuses, you shall take the ruby by force and run away.

I will wait for you at the edge of the forest, on the spot where the blue light of the sapphire shines. You must hurry!"

Aaron promised to follow the dwarf's instructions. Secretly, he took out the incredible outfit made of white satin, embroidered with silver. He found a hiding space near the exit, which was protected by the fern leaves, making it impossible to be seen.

Shortly after the other five dwarfs took off, the sixth one helped the boy get dressed, attached the sword, and checked all the decorations made of the finest jewels. He then provided him with the box made of amber and gold, inside of which a stunning diamond necklace was hidden. It was the 'trading' jewel for the princess's ruby.

This time, they headed straight to the main castle gate rather than using the secret passage. The dwarf accompanied Aaron, repeating the cunning plan in detail. He took off and left Aaron behind, feeling anxious and nervous.

Slowly, Aaron started to walk up the stairs, which were not just covered by a red carpet, but also by magnificent petals of fresh flowers of all possible colours. The staircase led to the dance hall. Beautiful music travelled all the way to the bottom of the stairs, inviting everyone in. The hall was breathtaking. A sea of lights was swimming in the reflection of all the mirrors that were covering the silver walls of the castle.

Aaron stood in the doorway looking around, feeling quite insecure, but the moment he spotted himself in the mirror, the fear was gone. He looked perfect, as dashing as any other prince in the room. Feeling confident and self-assured, he entered in pursuit of Princess Zora. He spotted her standing next to her sisters by her father's throne. She was staring sadly into the distance.

In a flash, Aaron was asking the princess to dance. She smiled and waited for her father's approval. Then she gave him her hand and started walking to the dance floor.

Everyone stopped dancing and stared at the couple in astonishment. All eyes were drawn to the beautiful couple.

Aaron danced the beautiful princess off her feet! He was whirling her so fast that the princess kindly requested a break as she could feel her head spinning. They walked to the park.

After walking for a while, they appeared at the spot where Aaron had been the night before. He told Princess Zora how he had seen her dancing with the small barefoot fairies that came out of the lotus flowers floating on the lake. Princess Zora froze, surprised that anyone would know about her magical spot, and asked to return to the castle. Aaron didn't move.

Princess Zora became enormously cross with Aaron when he would not obey her command to return. He quickly presented her with the amber and golden box and opened it so that the princess could see the necklace. The minute she saw all the shining diamonds, she fell in love with the necklace.

She grabbed it and started to play with it, carefully running to the lake. In the moonlight, she saw her reflection in the water.

"Gift me this necklace at once, and I will give you whatever you ask for!" she demanded.

Aaron asked for the ruby; but the princess refused. She offered all other possible treasures and jewels from the king's collection, but Aaron insisted on the ruby alone. She was furious and, in a rage, she threw the necklace into the lake.

The lake started to shake. Lotuses opened, and small pink fairies coughed up the diamond necklace and played with it, dancing over the waves. "What did you do that for?" shouted Aaron painfully as he realised that his little companion would not be happy if he returned without it, and without the ruby.

He started to move towards the princess, wanting to grab the ruby out of her beautiful black curls.

She looked up, begging him for forgiveness, and gently took the diamond necklace from the small fairies and placed it inside the amber and golden box. Seeing the kindness in her eyes, he was not capable of stealing the ruby the way it had been planned.

He did not return to the dancing hall with the princess. The king demanded to know who that fine dancer was, and her sisters demanded to know why he had left so suddenly. The princess was silent, though. She could not provide any answers.

Despite all of this, Princess Zora was determined to ask the young princely-looking boy who he was, were he to return. She knew that next time, she would not allow him to leave before he'd answered all her questions.

Aaron returned to the forest feeling glum. The blue light of the large sapphire was showing him the way and the golden curly-haired dwarf was nervously waiting for the boy, excited to learn of Aaron's success.

"Do you have it?" he asked, once he heard Aaron approaching.

"No," answered Aaron sadly.

"Did you follow all my instructions?"

"Yes, I followed them perfectly. However, the princess did not want to swap the ruby for the diamond necklace, despite loving it so much. And then I tried to steal the ruby with force, but she looked me straight in the eye, and I didn't have the strength to do it. I could not hurt her!"

"That's it, then!" the dwarf shook his head grumpily. "Hmm, now I see! You must bring me the ruby, regardless. You see, should you not complete the task, I will be ejected from my brothers' circle of trust. I have not brought any loot for two nights now, relying on you! Should I fail on a third night too, not presenting a great big treasure, I will be looking for a new home and will wander the Earth for eternity like a beggar!"

Aaron felt sorry for his beloved companion and he promised to go back and steal the ruby at once, no matter what.

"Should she ask you where you are from and where you live, you must not answer. You would reveal our hiding place and a curse would come upon us!" added the golden-curled dwarf before he laid down on his satin bedding in his little crystal room.

Dwarfs are magical creatures and must stay in magical hiding places away from the outside world. The two worlds know about each other and live side by side in harmony and alignment, with minimal interferences.

Once again, Aaron got his prince outfit ready. This one was more magnificent than the first. This time, the little dwarf had the amethyst box ready — a golden tiara of divine jewels. It looked like it was made of wildflowers, each flower made of a different coloured precious stone.

Once more, Aaron was instructed as follows: "You must convince the princess to exchange the magic ruby for this divine tiara. Should she refuse, you must take it from her with force!

Remember what an urgent situation I am in. Should you fail, I will end up evicted forever! Too much is at stake now!"

Aaron promised he would not fail this time and hurried away to the castle.

Upon his arrival, the king had just announced the feast. He sat down with all his daughters and invited Aaron to join the princesses. Aaron sat next to Princess Zora and started chatting away. The smell of roasted peacocks and suckling pigs wafted through the air. The sound of clinking glasses accompanied that amazing smell, and his heart was thumping as he spoke to Zora. All this beauty was interrupted by the king, who stepped out to the terrace with his daughters.

Aaron invited Princess Zora for a walk through the park, just like the last time. She quickly agreed, as she was desperate to find out more about this mysterious boy — where he came from, where he lived and what his name was.

Aaron was avoiding the answers and reluctantly agreed to share his secret if — and only if — she agreed to exchange the ruby for the truly divine tiara he had brought with him.

"Show me what you offer in exchange," demanded the princess, and curiously peeked inside the amethyst box.

There, on the sparkling bed of gold and jewels of various colours, lay the extraordinary tiara! Princess Zora could not hide her astonishment even if she'd wanted to. She slowly started to take the ruby out of her beautiful hair. Then suddenly, she froze and thought for a second.

"Do you know why I cannot be parted from my precious jewel?" she asked. "I do not love it for its beauty and price. I am attached to it for far more valuable reasons. Its magical powers are given to every single person wearing it.

If I give it to you, I will not understand the language of the lotus flowers that open every night. I will not understand the stories that leaves on trees tell each other lovingly when they meet in the breeze or wind. My father and sisters cannot see how I can read their minds and know their deepest inner secrets. All secrets and treasures are revealed to me in the realm of the ruby. And that is the divine ultimate beauty of life!"

"If your jewel is so precious, why doesn't it answer the questions you seek and reveal my thoughts and secrets?" wondered Aaron aloud.

"I do not know. I cannot understand it. Possibly, you are not of this Earth if my ruby can't read your rhythm. If you answer my questions, the ruby is yours!" said Princess Zora firmly, and she took her precious ruby out of her hair. She held it in front of her with her palms open so that Aaron could see.

Out of the bushes by the road where they were standing, the little golden-haired dwarf rustled out slowly, begging Aaron with his eyes and hands to steal the jewel from the princess.

Aaron's little friend's begging eyes tugged anxiously at his heart, and in that moment, invisible mist blinded his mind and thinking. He grabbed the ruby and ran away. Princess Zora started screaming and followed Aaron. She could not keep up as Aaron and his little companion mysteriously disappeared behind the tall wall by the park.

Aaron started slowing down as they were reaching the forest. However, the little dwarf encouraged him to keep running. He was afraid of the Royal Guard. And he was right! The king and the Royal Guard rushed to the gardens when they heard the princess's cry. When she told them about her precious ruby that the trusted boy had stolen, the king rose up like a tall mountain.

He gave orders to ride the finest and fastest horses to find the mysterious knight who dared to steal the princess's special ruby with his insolent hand!

Aaron and the little dwarf had barely reached the rocks when they heard a thunder of hooves, which hit them like a strong wind above their heads. They arrived at the opening and breathlessly managed to slip into the underground through the magic protective entrance. The last they heard was the angry gallop of the Royal Guard returning from their unsuccessful expedition.

Aaron did not need to worry as he was now safe and protected in the underground. Yet, he did not join his companions in celebrating their success, and his heart ached with sorrow.

He closed his eyes gently and imagined Princess Zora and her kindness and love. She was beautiful inside and out, and the picture of her wearing the tiara with its sparkling precious jewels and Cupid's love dust flying around her stunning dress completed this vision in Aaron's mind.

The image of her was perfection and it lit up Aaron's heart and soul with a warmth that travelled everywhere in the underground. It was the most beautiful dream state Aaron had ever been in. Suddenly, he opened his eyes, and the splendid vision disappeared.

At nighttime, when all the dwarfs traditionally set off on a mission, Aaron stayed underground, pretending to be very tired. Shortly after they left, he took the precious ruby out of his pocket and sneaked out through the enormous fern bush, following the already-known path all the way to the city wall. Through the broken loophole, he jumped on the branches of the massive oak tree and slid down the mist straight to the park, to the place he knew.

He felt strange while taking the path. It was like something was calling him. It was the ruby!
With every touch, he connected to the heart of the precious jewel.

The soothing breeze of the gentle wind was like soul-calming music to his mind. The leaves were talking to each other, the flowers reaching out to Aaron, telling him of Princess Zora's sadness. They told him of her tears and broken heart, of her despair at losing her precious ruby, as well as the one who took it from her.

Suddenly, a large lily bent over a row of beautiful white roses and whispered into Aaron's ear, "Princess Zora does not wish to punish the brave robber. She wants to forgive him if he comes back."

The white roses happily shook off their white petals as if they agreed with the graceful lily. Pink fairies jumped out from lotus flowers and rushed to make soft beds out of the white petals. They lay down smiling.

Aaron returned to the magicalunderground and he was calm and felt joyful again. He was grateful to the flowers for telling him that the princess was not mad and would gladly forgive him if he returned.

Before everyone arrived back, he rushed to the underground treasury to replace the ruby in its exact spot so nobody would discover it had been taken for a bit.

He turned and rushed to leave when, out of nowhere, the littlest dwarf, his closest friend, stood in front of him with a frown and cracked his whip.

"I knew curiosity would win. It was stronger than you, wasn't it? Although, why on Earth would you secretly set off to the castle and risk your life? Don't you know that the king has not stopped looking for you and that he'll kill you when he captures you?"

Aaron bent his head down and tears fell from his eyes. That softened the little dwarf, and he promised to do everything in his power to make Aaron happy again. Aaron revealed a secret to his little companion, that he was in love with the princess. The little dwarf nodded and thought about it for a considerably long time. That night, he sought the advice of the others.

Early in the morning, all the dwarfs sent Aaron off to the castle. They dressed him up, this time not in the finest clothes, but the poorest ones they could find. They gave him the princess's precious ruby and reminded him to return it to Princess Zora. "You must tell her the truth about your story and your childhood in poverty. She needs to know your true story. Then you ask her to marry you."

Aaron made futile attempts to persuade them not to send him to the king in his poor clothes. Eventually, he yielded and headed for the castle, accompanied by his companions and their wise counsel.

This time, he was not walking proudly. He felt shame, disgrace, and fear of rejection. He was afraid he would not be enough for the princess once she found out he was not the mysterious knight she thought he was. "She will never look at me the same way and will want nothing to do with me ever!" feared Aaron. His heart was pumping hard and the mist of fear was filling the space around him.

To his surprise, he was mistaken. Princess Zora caught sight of Aaron from her balcony the minute he entered the courtyard, and she ran to welcome him with the biggest smile. Her heart filled with joy. She took Aaron to the king, showed him the returned ruby and demanded of him that she become Aaron's wife.

"I will give you the hand of my youngest daughter, Zora, on one condition. Your wealth and riches must match mine!" said the king firmly. Aaron lost heart, and did not dare respond.

Princess Zora begged her father to call off his decision, but to no avail. The king demanded the princess be taken to her chambers and ordered that diligent guards be placed on all routes leading to her. "In case the princess feels like escaping," the king added.

Aaron returned to his underground companions and told them what had happened.

The dwarfs sang the praises of Princess Zora and sat discussing the matter with each other for a while.

Then they set out to work. They started collecting all their gold, treasures, jewels and diamonds, putting them in sacks and taking them out onto the glade. Once they'd emptied their entire treasury, they called Aaron and gave him one sack to carry. Each of them put a sack on the wheelbarrow and dashed off to the castle.

The king smiled, seeing Aaron approaching with such peculiar companions, each carrying a sack. He called for the princess.

"Look at him." The king pointed his finger at Aaron, mocking his attempt at courtship with a sack over his shoulder. The princess's sisters were laughing at Aaron too, although secretly they were jealous of her handsome suitor.

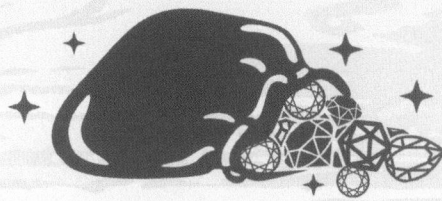

Aaron walked into the hall, proudly followed by his magical companions. They laid all the sacks on the floor in front of Princess Zora and stepped back. The king ordered Aaron to open the sacks, still mocking the kind of "treasure" that could be hiding in such hideously thick sacks.

He immediately froze with astonishment. Out of the sacks poured the finest jewels, diamonds, gold and expensive trinkets the king's eye had ever seen. The whole room hushed to a whisper. Those mocking fell silent and jeering laughter was replaced by open-mouthed wonder.

The first sack alone exceeded all the king's wealth and treasure. Yet, when Aaron opened the rest and showed the princess gleaming tiaras, clips, bands, beautiful sparkling ornaments made from gold, diamonds and jewels, rare pearls and precious rocks, it left everyone in the room impressed beyond measure.

But this was not all, for the last sack contained hidden treasure: the most exquisite wedding dress and veil anyone had ever seen! The king was simply stunned. Princess Zora's sisters were jealous and secretly cross with themselves for mocking their sister. Now they were left with nothing.

The room filled with joy and cheers as the king shared his sudden change of heart. He gave Zora and Aaron his blessing to be married that day. The happiest, richest of all were Zora and Aaron and their true, unending love.

The magical dwarfs never returned to their underground world. They stayed in the castle protecting their special companion and the treasures that sealed his happiness.

THE END

About The Author

Vladimira Kuna is the Slovak-born International Best-Selling Author of "The Bible of The Masterminds" and currently lives in the UK. Her two abundant and open-minded children, Joshua and Elizabeth, have unleashed her hidden power of writing. She is in love with personal growth, writing books, traveling, serving others and finds joy in the life she has chosen – and that has chosen her!

Vladimira is also a Belief & Self-Mastery Mentor and is extremely passionate about helping others fulfill their dreams. On her phenomenal journey, mindset coaching became her life purpose and the growth she is experiencing while helping others is simply priceless.

Vladimira is also a climber & mountaineer and loves adventure & nature. Vladimira is in love with climbing both physical and mental mountains and finds joy in her journey every step of the way. She is grateful for having become an author and coach and loves who she became in the process.

At the time of this publication, Vladimira is writing her third book and has three more fairy-tales to write that will compliment this amazing story.

Vladimira is known for her loving heart, and cares extremely for everyone – especially children. She really believes there is abundance everywhere and pure love is the TRUE core to all there is.

Feel free to reach out with any comments or stories of your own to share:
WWW.VLADIMIRAKUNA.COM
and follow @vladimirakuna on Facebook, Instagram, YouTube, Twitter, TikTok and LinkedIn.

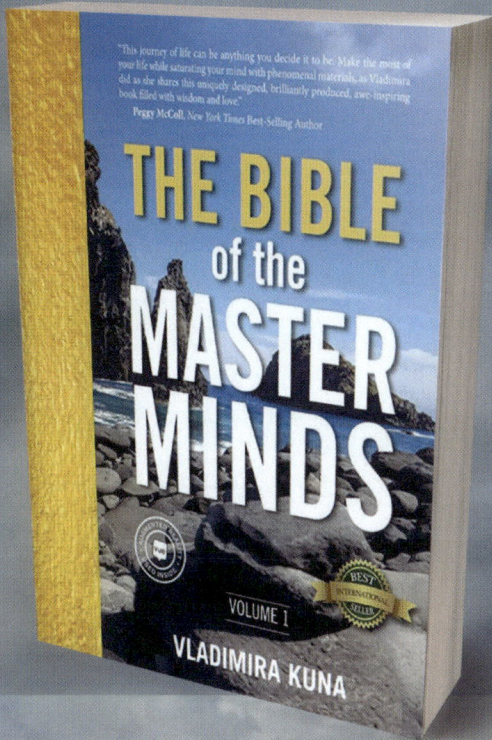

A MESSAGE FROM THE AUTHOR ABOUT THE SPECIAL ORIGINS OF THIS BOOK

I am honoured and feel very privileged to re-tell four amazing stories with such important moral messages; this book is the first of these four stories.

Marie Calma is the Czechoslovakian author of the original story, which she gifted to me and entrusted me to breathe light into again.

I am so delighted and grateful to acknowledge and honour this amazing and powerful woman. Thank you Marie!

MARIE CALMA

8. SEPTEMBER 1881 - 7. APRIL 1966

She was the wife of the director of the spa, MUDr. František Veselý. She spent two seasons in Luhačovice and advocated the creation of a spa newspaper and the development of cultural events. She has done a lot for Luhačovice during her short-term work. Marie Calma Veselá was a singer, poet, writer, modern woman. Alongside her husband, she immediately became involved in cultural life in Luhačovice. For example, she initiated the creation of Luhačovice spa leaves, which were published twice a week under her direction and published by the spa doctor Zikmund Janke. In 1909, on the occasion of the opening of the Bedřich Smetana House, she organized a large Smetana Music Festival, which had an unprecedented response. On the day of her twenty-seventh birthday, September 8, 1908, she met the composer Leoš Janáček. This meeting and the establishment of friendship was of great importance for Janáček. The Veselí couple helped the composer to promote his musical works in Prague.

Acknowledgements

To my most abundant children Joshua and Elizabeth. You rock my world, and I am complete by being your mother! I love you infinity x infinity and I am so proud of you both and of who you are becoming. You inspire me every day to be better and greater.

To my husband Peter for continuous support and love. And to all my family for the greatest journey ever!

To my amazing mentor and friend Peggy McColl, thank you for your great wisdom and your belief in me, your guidance to be a better and greater person and author. I love and appreciate you.

To Phillip B. Goldfine, Film Television & Broadway Producer. Thank you for your belief in me and your incredible support in my growth. I deeply appreciate you.

To Martin and Sergey, my friends who gifted me this lost book and encouraged me to bring it to the world's light again.

To my friend and growth "buddy" Trace Haskins, thank you for helping me to put this amazing book together and to support and guide me sharing knowledge and amazing skills of yours. I am so happy and grateful to know you.

To my beautiful friend Renata Natale for showing up like an angel and helping me turn this manuscript into the proper version at the last minute. Really grateful.

To Yorris Handoko for amazing illustrations, great support and flexibility. Thank you for capturing the story in these breathtakingly beautiful illustrations.

To Hasmark Publishing International for all of your amazing work and support with publishing. I appreciate you, always!

To Norman, Jonna, Roddy, Clare, Michelle, Gena and Sara for being the "Soulmates" in my life. Love and appreciate you more than words can say.

Finally, a very special feeling of gratitude and love to all readers and supporters. I intend for this book to touch your hearts and for you to to enjoy the deep meaning behind this moral story.

Printed in Great Britain
by Amazon